BEASTS OF OLYMPUS

CENTAUR SCHOOL

LUCY COATS

with illustrations by
David Roberts

Piccadilly
PRESS

First published in Great Britain in 2016
by Piccadilly Press
80–81 Wimpole Street, London W1G 9RE
www.piccadillypress.co.uk

A CIP catalogue record for this book
is available from the British Library

ISBN: 978–1–84812–530–8
1 3 5 7 9 10 8 6 4 2

Typeset by Palimpsest Book Production Limited,
Falkirk, Stirlingshire

FSC

Printed and bound in Great Britain by Clays Ltd, St Ives plc

Piccadilly Press is an imprint of the Bonnier Publishing Fiction,
a Bonnier Publishing company
www.bonnierpublishingfiction.co.uk
www.bonnierpublishing.co.uk

For Michelle Lovric, with love and phoenixes

1

ITCHY ARNIE

Since Colin the Colchian Dragon had nearly exploded Olympus with the seriously stinky gas from his poorly stomach, Demon had learned oodles and squoodles of useful stuff about mixing medicines and proper animal doctoring from his teacher, the centaur god Chiron, but there was one thing he just couldn't seem to get right.

'AARRRGGHH!' The Official Beastkeeper to the Gods and Apprentice Healer stood up, threw down the slate he was writing on and stamped on it. Twice. He looked at the book that lay open beside him on the bale of silver hay. The letters beside the beautiful pictures on the pages were all wriggly and squirly and squiggly. His own attempts to copy them were even worse. 'I'm NEVER going to learn to write properly,' he said, sitting down again with a despairing thump.

A large beak reached down from the roof of the Stables of the Gods and nipped his ear.

'What's up, Pan's scrawny kid?' asked Arnie, flapping down into the light of another bright Olympus day. 'Why the long face? You look as grumpy as the Giant Scorpion.' The griffin sat down on its lion's rump and began to scratch under its wing feathers with one sharp-clawed back paw.

'Chiron says I have to make notes on all my new patients,' Demon replied. 'But the letters won't stay still. They all wiggle and try to run away when I read them, AND when I write them down. It's giving me a headache as horrid as Hera in a huff.'

Arnie scratched some more. 'Sounds like a

puzzle for old Heffy to me,' it said. 'Why not go on up to the forge and ask him what to do about it?'

Demon looked around him. He'd worked extra hard to get the stables spick and span that morning. All the immortal beasts were cleaned out and munching on ambrosia cake or sun hay – and he wasn't due down at Chiron the centaur's cave for his lesson till later.

'Good idea,' he said. Then he frowned at the griffin. 'Stop scratching. You'll make yourself bleed.' But Arnie just turned its eagle head round and used the pointy tip of its beak to scratch even harder.

'I've got an itch,' it said sulkily. 'Not that you care, running off to earth all the time like you do now.'

Demon rolled his eyes. 'I'll ask Chiron what ointment to mix up for you,' he said.

'Why not ask that magic medicine box of yours?' Arnie asked. 'No need to trouble your teacher.'

Demon sighed.

'I can't,' he said. 'Chiron's forbidden it to help me – at least till I've learned much more about proper healing,' he said. 'But he's already taught me loads and loads of things, so don't worry. I'll bring something back with me tonight.'

'You'd better,' said the griffin, swishing its tail. 'Or else.'

As he set off up the mountain to visit the blacksmith god Hephaestus, his book under one arm, Demon wondered nervously what Arnie's 'or else' might mean. He'd been on the wrong side of a few griffin wounds by now – and they hurt.

A long arrow-pointed tail, covered in bright purple scales, snaked out of the smith god's forge. Demon carefully sidestepped it and poked his head round the door.

Hephaestus was standing by Colin the Colchian Dragon, scratching it behind the horns with his grimy fingers. The dragon's eyes were closed in bliss, and happy orangey-purple jewel tears were rolling down its face, dropping with tiny plinks on to the grimy floor, where they shone like miniature stars.

'Good dragon,' said the blacksmith god encouragingly. 'Just a few more and I'll have enough for Hera's new tiara. Then you can have as much charcoal as you can eat.'

Demon eyed the dragon's bulk. If Colin ate much more charcoal, he reckoned Hephaestus would have to get a bigger forge. But he wasn't going to suggest that the beast went on a diet. The memory of its terrible farting problem and how it had nearly blown up the whole of Olympus was still too fresh in his memory. Just then, Hephaestus turned round and saw him.

'Hello, young Pandemonius! What's up?'

After Demon had explained, Hephaestus tapped one grubby nail against his teeth, thinking.

'Young Eros had just the same trouble,' he said. 'Aphrodite kept after me for months to sort him out after he spelled some love letters all wrong and nearly started a war.' He chuckled. 'He's a little scamp, is Eros. Him and his love potions. Always some poor girl or boy with hearts coming out of their ears.'

Hephaestus went over to a wooden box, rummaged around and came back holding some thick golden wire and dusty square blocks of blue, pink and yellow crystal, which he cleaned off with a damp rag.

'What are those for?' Demon asked, to the accompaniment of loud, happy crunching sounds in the background as chubby Colin munched on a trough full of charcoal.

'You'll see,' said Hephaestus, setting them down on his workbench. Working fast, he twisted and turned the wire in his big, grimy hands, until he had a strange-looking frame, with two attached circles and two long arms. Then he carefully tapped each block of crystal with a small silver hammer until he had three thin, transparent sheets of different colours. He beckoned to Demon. 'Give me the book.' Demon handed it over, and quickly, the smith god opened it and laid a sheet of blue crystal over the page. 'Have a look,' he ordered.

Demon looked. The letters were just as squiggly as ever. He shook his head. Hephaestus whipped the blue crystal away and replaced it with the yellow. Demon shook his head again. Yellow made his stomach want to heave.

'I don't think it's working,' he said. A little knot of despair was growing inside him. If the letters didn't behave, he'd never be able to be a proper apprentice healer to Chiron.

'Don't give up yet, boy,' said the smith god. He laid the pink crystal down and, suddenly, everything on the page became still and clear.

'Oh!' said Demon, staring at the straight, elegant lines of writing. 'It's like magic!'

'Not magic this time,' said Hephaestus, looking smug underneath his huge black beard. 'Just godly cleverness.'

He took one of the dragon's jewel tears and used its sharp point to cut two little circles out of the pink crystal, fixing them tightly within the circles on the golden wire frame. Then he popped them on Demon's nose and fastened the arms behind his ears. After making a few adjustments, he stood back.

'There you are,' he said. 'Problem solved! I call them opticles.'

With the opticles on, Demon's world was now slightly pink-tinted, but he didn't care. Now he could take proper notes! Chiron would be happy. Just to be sure though, he grabbed a piece of chalk and one of the slates Hephaestus used to scrawl designs on.

Demon was here, he wrote in slightly wobbly letters, under a picture of a new automaton.

'Get along with you!' Hephaestus said, snatching the slate back and shooing him down the mountain.

When Demon got off the Iris Express rainbow and went into the light, airy cave to find his teacher, neither Chiron nor his assistant, Asclepius, were anywhere to be seen. However, he could hear a strange noise in the distance, a sort of snorty, shouty sound and some high screaming. Maybe an animal was in trouble and the centaur god had gone to heal it. He ran outside to see.

At first there was nothing, only the usual silvery cistus and olive trees waving in the breeze, with the blue of King Poseidon's realm down below. But then, round the corner of a rock, came a tall, thin young man, running so fast that he was past Demon and into the cave before Demon could do more than gasp. Behind him, in a cloud of white dust, galloped a crowd of about twenty centaurs. Unlike Chiron, these weren't nice calm centaurs. Oh no! These centaurs were angry, with rolling red eyes and bared white teeth and rearing hooves that pounded the ground so hard that it shook.

Demon threw himself into a bush just in time, as a plate-sized hoof slapped through the air exactly where his head had been.

'Whoa!' he said breathlessly, his heart thumping harder than a hammer on an anvil. 'What's going on?' But nobody heard him. The herd of centaurs milled about in front of the cave, stamping angrily and swishing their tails like vicious fly swats. In their hands he could see torn-off branches and slings full of rocks.

'Peleus!' they screamed. 'Prince Peleus! Come out and die!'

Demon eyed the angry mob. Things weren't looking too good for this Prince Peleus, whoever he was.

'Suppose I'd better go and help,' he muttered, pushing the bag that held his book and the precious opticles into the space between two rocks.

He crawled through the bushes on his belly to avoid being seen, slipped round a corner and squeezed into Chiron's cave by one of the small round windows carved into the side of the mountain. As he landed, a body shot out from under one of the empty beds and tackled him to the ground, pinning his arms over his head with two strong hands.

'Oof!' Demon grunted. 'Get off me! I've come to help!'

Two very green eyes looked at him down a long, thin nose, before letting him up.

'Bit small for a warrior, aren't you?' said Prince Peleus scornfully, flicking back his straight, black hair. 'Where's your sword? You can't stab those centaurs without a sword.'

Demon dusted himself down before replying. He was fed up with people thinking that everything could be sorted out with swords and violence.

'I'm not a warrior,' he said crossly. 'And I don't need a sword.' Without another word, he marched to the front of the cave, pulling out his father's silver pipes from the front of his tunic. Putting them to his lips, he blew a long, discordant blast that echoed off the rocks, bouncing back and forth like shrill thunder.

'Oi! You lot!' he shouted. 'Shut up and listen'.

It was as if a sheet of perfect silence had fallen over the mountain. Not a bird sang, not a cricket chirped.

Then the lead centaur snorted, red foam dripping from his lips.

'Who are you, boy? And what are you doing with Pan's pipes? Just wait till he catches you! He'll tear you apart with his teeth.'

'Pan's my dad,' sad Demon. 'And he gave them to me, so there. Now, what do you want with Prince Peleus?'

As if the name had lit a fire under them, the centaurs began to scream and rear and shout once more. Demon was just about to blow his dad's pipes again, when a great voice shouted from the back of the herd.

'STOP THAT RACKET AT ONCE!'

The centaurs all wheeled round and fell to their knees.

Chiron had arrived.

2

THE LOST SWORD

Demon watched admiringly as Chiron sent the centaur herd trotting away after giving them a good telling-off for daring to trespass on his mountain. He didn't allow them to say a single thing other than 'Yes, Chiron', 'No, Chiron' and 'Sorry, Chiron'. By the time he had finished with them, their heads were low and their tails were drooping. Then he turned to Demon, tossing him a large sack full of strong-smelling herbs.

'By Zeus's toenails, young Pandemonius! What's been happening here?'

Demon caught it, wrinkling his nose and trying not to sneeze.

'I don't know. I was just trying to calm them down. They were chasing him.' He jerked a thumb over his shoulder at Prince Peleus, who stepped forward from the shadows with a swagger, and shouldered his way past Demon to stand in front of the centaur god.

Chiron's bushy eyebrows lowered.

'Young Peleus,' he growled. 'What trouble have you got yourself into now, grandson?'

Peleus shrugged sulkily.

'I was only looking for my sword, Grandpa,' he said. 'I came up here on a hunting trip with my friend Acastus. But we had a big argument last night. The stupid idiot stole my sword and hid it from me, then he led me into a trap. Who knew that interrupting a centaur ceremony was such a big deal?'

Chiron's brows lowered even further.

'Was there a big golden bowl involved? And a sheaf of grain?'

Peleus nodded.

'I only knocked their silly bowl over, and scattered their grain when I ran into their glade,' he said, crossing his arms defiantly. 'I don't know why they got all upset — I was going to pick it up but those big bullies never even gave me a chance.'

'You were lucky they didn't trample you into tiny little pieces,' the centaur god said, snorting.

'Well, I'm sorry,' said Peleus, not sounding it at all, Demon thought. 'But I had to get my sword back.' He stamped his foot. 'I HAD to!'

'What's so special about your sword?' Demon asked. 'Can't you just get another one? They're all pretty much the same, aren't they?'

Peleus whirled round.

'Stupid little boy,' he snapped, putting his long nose in the air in a way that made Demon want to give him to the Giant Scorpion for an afternoon. 'Don't you know anything? It's a magic sword,

Hermes gave it to me. It makes me invincible in battle.'

Suddenly the air grew close and hot, and Demon felt as if a thousand angry wasps were buzzing in the air around him and Peleus.

'WHERE ARE YOUR MANNERS, SON OF MY DAUGHTER?' Chiron thundered, in a voice that made it obvious he was Zeus's brother. Then, slightly more quietly, 'Pandemonius was brave enough to face down those centaurs for you, young man. Do you really think you should be calling my Apprentice Healer a "stupid little boy"? I don't think he's the one who's been stupid!'

Peleus hung his head, blushing.

'Sorry,' he said, and this time he sounded like he meant it. Then he held out a hand to Demon.

Demon shook it, a warm glow starting somewhere round his heart. Chiron really was on his side, even when the god's own family was involved. It felt good. He was more used to gods threatening to turn him into things – most often a little pile of burnt charcoal.

'Now,' said the centaur god, patting his grandson on the shoulder. 'Come and help me hang the herbs up to dry, both of you, and then we can see about finding this sword.'

A few hours later, Demon was beginning to wish he'd let those centaurs have Peleus. Instead of his precious healing lesson with Chiron, he'd been stumbling about all over the mountain with Peleus, looking for his wretched magic sword. Listening to the centaur god's grandson as he stood around boasting about how many soldiers he'd knocked down in his training session, and how being a prince was the way to get girls wasn't really Demon's idea of a fun day out. Nor was poking his hands into holes till his fingers were black with dirt and climbing trees till his knees were skinned and bloody. It wasn't as bad as being bitten by his beasts, but it wasn't far off. Luckily, Offy and Yukus, the golden snakes from his magic necklace, had sorted out the cuts and bruises quite quickly.

'I wonder if I should tell Chiron about you

two,' he whispered, feeling a bit guilty. 'You heard him say I'm not supposed to use magic to heal things any more. Heffy made you two, just like he made my box.'

'We'd advissse ssstaying sssilent,' hissed the snakes. 'Chiron doesssn't need to know.'

'Well, if you really think so,' said Demon, peering into yet another rabbit burrow.

'We do,' they said, slithering round his neck again, and curling their tails together.

By the time they got back to Chiron's cave, both he and Peleus were tired and hungry, and neither of them had found the sword. Demon looked anxiously at the sky. Helios's sun chariot had nearly driven over the horizon. It was time for him to call the Iris Express and go home to Olympus to feed Arnie and the other beasts their evening ambrosia cake.

'Oh no!' he said, smacking himself in the head. 'I forgot Arnie's ointment.'

'Who's Arnie?' Peleus asked.

'My . . . I mean . . . Zeus's griffin,' he said.

'He's got a terrible itch in his feathers and I was supposed to make something to cure it today. Only with looking for your sword and everything, I haven't exactly had time.'

He went into the cave to find Chiron. The centaur god was humming to himself as he lit the beeswax candles around his surgery with a flick of his fingers, making the shadows sway and retreat into the corners.

'Can you tell me what to use for itchy griffin feathers, please?' Demon asked. 'We haven't done that yet.'

'Itchy griffin feathers? Did you take a proper patient history? Did you write down times and symptoms on your slate like I showed you?'

'No,' Demon confessed. 'I've had a bit of trouble with the reading and writing. But it's fine now I've got Hephaestus's opticles,' he added hastily.

'Well, go back and do it properly,' said his teacher, reaching for a large jar and pouring some dried daisy heads into a little bag. 'Meanwhile crush these up and sprinkle the powder on him. It's probably only feather mites. Work it well in with a brush, mind, so it covers the whole area.'

'When did the itching start?' Demon asked, the opticles perched on the end of his nose and his slate propped against his knees. He'd fed and mucked out all the beasts as well as pounding the daisy heads to a fine dust, and now he was sitting on the floor in Arnie's pen. The griffin was looking rather sour as it pecked half-heartedly at a large slab of ambrosia cake.

'Dunno,' it said. 'Yesterday? Day before? Why's it matter anyway, Pan's scrawny kid?'

'Because Chiron says I have to find out and write it down, that's why. Now tell me what kind of itch it is? Prickly? Hot? Burning?'

Arnie looked at him out of one large, golden eye.

'An itchy itch is what it is. Now have you got something for it or not? Because if you haven't I'd appreciate being left alone to eat my dinner and scratch.' It picked up the slab in its beak and dropped it on the floor, spraying Demon with small particles of stale ambrosia. 'Not that I fancy it tonight. Or any night really. Disgusting stuff.'

Demon sighed. He agreed with Arnie. Ambrosia was the food of the gods, and it had given him really strong muscles and made him grow much taller since he'd been eating it – but he'd much rather have one of Hestia's honey cakes; they were his all-time favourites.

'Come on, then,' he said. 'Spread out your wings. I need to get the powder right into the feathers.'

Soon every griffin feather was covered in a greyish-green powder. Demon couldn't see any mites running about, but that didn't mean they weren't there.

'All done,' he said, patting Arnie's rough lion's pelt. 'That should fix it. You'll be fine by the morning.'

★

When Demon crawled out from under his spider-silk blanket the next day, he whistled happily as he clattered down the ladder at dawn. Doris the Hydra was waiting for him, buckets, brooms and pitchforks dangling from its nine mouths, all ready to help him with his cleaning duties.

'Morning, Doris,' he said cheerfully. 'Extra snackies if you can help me muck out in double-quick time. I want to get down to Chiron's cave early today.' The Hydra fluttered its curly eyelashes and began to drool. But as Demon wheeled the poo barrow up the stables towards where the Cattle of the Sun were mooing for their breakfast of sun hay, he became aware of a low, angry growling sound coming from Arnie's pen. Cautiously, he unlatched it and poked his head round the door.

At once, a huge, sharp beak lashed out at him, making him jump back and slam it shut.

'WRETCHED BOY!' roared Arnie. 'LOOK AT MY FEATHERS!'

Demon stood on tiptoe and peered in cautiously. The griffin had retreated to a corner, where it crouched in a huddle, its tail lashing furiously. The draught it caused was making a whole pillowful of shed feathers whirl and flutter into the air. The griffin's wings had holes in them, and, almost worse, the tiny golden feathers on its eagle head had fallen off in great clumps, leaving pink bald patches with bright purple spots behind them.

'Oh, *Arnie* . . .' Demon began.

But the griffin was in no mood for sympathy.

'You're going to pay for this, Pan's scrawny kid,' it hissed, hurling itself at the bars.

3

FEATHER DILEMMA

Demon was almost in tears as he leapt back from the pen. Had the daisy powder done this? Surely Arnie knew that he'd never hurt him – or any beast – deliberately? Nor would Chiron. It was all some terrible mistake, and he needed to fix it. This was an emergency. He had to hope Chiron wouldn't mind if he used his magic medicine box now. Despite all he'd learned from his centaur teacher, he had no idea what was wrong with the griffin – or how to cure it.

Running like one of Artemis's golden deer, he pelted out of the stables and over to the hospital shed. The medicine box lay in the corner, its silvery sides looking a little tarnished and dusty. He banged his hand on the lid.

'Wake up, box! Arnie's feathers are falling out. I need you! It's an emergency!'

For a second, his heart leapt as the box glowed blue. But then a big red cross flowed over its top and sides.

'Closed for business until further notice,' it said in its metallic voice. Then it went dark.

'Nooo!' Demon wailed, running his hands through his curly hair till it stood on end like a messy brown bottle-brush. What was he going to do? He scrabbled through the cupboards, trying to think of anything he could use to help the griffin. Then his hand brushed against something cold – a big copper tub with a stopper.

'Yes!' he whispered. 'The ointment I used on King Poseidon's hippocamps to stop the Persistent Itchy-itch.' Quickly, he took it down. Feathers weren't that different from scales, were they? Maybe it would help. He opened it, then groaned. The jar was only a quarter full. It would have to do, though. He had nothing else till he could get down to Chiron. Clutching it to his chest, he ran back to the stables.

By this time, all the other beasts were clamouring for their morning meal. The noise was deafening.

'I'm coming! I'm coming!' he called. 'But I need to sort out poor Arnie first. Please be quiet – you know how Aphrodite gets if she misses her beauty sleep.' As the racket died down a bit, he thought back to the week before and winced. The beautiful goddess had threatened to make him fall in love with the Giant Scorpion after there had been a particularly loud early-morning bellowing battle between the three fire-breathing bulls. They had had an argument over which one of them was strongest, and nearly set the whole stables alight.

Demon took a deep breath and went into Arnie's pen. Even more feathers had fallen off the poor beast now, and his feet made shushing noises as he waded through them. The griffin's eyes were closed, and it was making distressed little whiffling noises through its beak. As soon as he got close though, it reared up and tried to scratch him.

'Stop it,' he said, dodging the huge claws. 'I'm trying to help.'

'It had better be more successful than your last effort, Pan's scrawny kid,' the griffin spat. 'Or I'll be taking off your fingers and toes one by one. See how you manage then.'

By the time he'd finished spreading the sticky goop on, Arnie's top half looked more like a bedraggled chicken than a fierce eagle.

'Is it helping the itching?' he asked.

The griffin nodded.

'A bit,' it growled. 'But you need to stick my feathers on again, like you did with the pegasi. Or regrow them. I can't go about looking like this. And I can't fly either. They'll all laugh at me out there, just you wait and see.' Arnie looked thoroughly miserable.

'Tell you what,' said Demon. 'There are some

nice airy pens out at the back of the hospital shed. I've never used them, but I think they're meant for any beast that has something the others might catch. Chiron's been teaching me about infections. I don't know if you've got one, but it's best to be safe. You can go in one of those and no one will be able to see you while you get better.'

Arnie looked at him in its usual sly manner.

'I'm not hungry at the moment, but I might need a special diet,' it said hopefully. 'Some nice minced lamb with blood gravy and a sprinkle of scarab beetles. That would make my feathers pop up in no time.'

'We'll see,' said Demon. 'Let's get those purple spots to go away first.'

By the time he reached Chiron's cave again, Demon was more tired than a dormouse who's run a marathon. He'd fed and cleaned in double-quick time, moved Arnie to his new pen, and, after washing his hands thoroughly, had checked the winged pegasi and the Caucasian Eagle for any signs of feather drop and itching. Luckily, they all seemed fine.

Chiron was waiting for him, tapping one front hoof impatiently on the earth.

'Where have you been? I don't expect my apprentice to be late. It's bad enough that Asclepius has gone off to tend that new wife of his. I'm snowed under with mortal patients.' He frowned down at Demon.

'I-I'm sorry,' Demon stammered. 'It's Arnie. I don't know what to do . . .' He consulted his slate and read out the griffin's symptoms, then looked up at Chiron. 'I'm calling it the Purple Spotted Feather Plague,' he said.

'Hmm,' said the centaur god. 'Purple spots, you say. And extreme feather drop. Did you say decreased appetite too?'

Demon nodded.

'Do you know what it is, then?' he asked. 'What should I treat it with? Only Arnie's threatened to bite off all my fingers and toes if I don't find something quickly.'

Chiron gave a sort of strangled cough. Demon looked at him suspiciously. Was his teacher laughing at him? Didn't he realise how serious the situation was? It was no good trying to be a healer with no digits.

'It's definitely an infection, so you did the right thing by isolating the griffin from the other feathered beasts,' Chiron said. 'You'll need to get anything with feathers away from Olympus, just to be safe. I suggest you tell the Caucasian Eagle to roost in the mountains when he's finished tearing out poor old Prometheus's liver today – and I suppose the pegasi herd can come down here. They'll like a bit of a holiday, I expect.'

Demon was still very worried.

'It's . . . it's not, well . . . fatal, is it?' he asked, a big bumpy throat lump making his words hard to get out. He didn't think he could bear it if Arnie died.

Chiron laughed out loud this time.

'Use that brain of yours, young healer! Arnie's an immortal beast. He might be very sick, but he won't die. The worst that could happen is that Zeus will make him into a set of stars — but he only does that to beasts who've done something to help us gods, not just to an ordinary griffin.'

'So what medicine do I use?' Demon asked.

The centaur god shook a green-stained finger at him.

'No, no, Pandemonius. I'm not going to tell you what to treat Arnie with. It's time you worked things out by yourself. I'd start by looking up "I for Itching" in the big book with the red thread round it.' The centaur stamped a hoof and reached for his healer's bag, slinging it over one brown, muscled shoulder. 'I'll leave you to it, then, my young apprentice. I'm off to see a patient in the village below — with Asclepius away, I've got more work than I can handle. Why they decided to have a baby, I can't imagine. It's very inconvenient.'

Muttering crossly, he trotted off down the mountain, leaving Demon staring after him with his mouth open. He couldn't work out whether he was annoyed at being left, or flattered that

Chiron finally trusted him to come up with a remedy all on his own.

He put on his opticles and pulled the book down from the shelf, muttering to himself as he sounded out the difficult words. By the time he'd got to the end, he was thoroughly confused. Even wearing Heffy's invention he still wasn't very fast at reading yet, and there seemed to be about a hundred kinds of itching, all with different cures – and none of them was exactly like Arnie's. He went outside to give his brain a rest, and bumped straight into a rather bedraggled-looking Prince Peleus, who was sitting on a rock gloomily picking bits of twig out of his hair.

'Still no luck with the sword?' Demon asked.

Peleus shook his head.

'I've looked everywhere,' he said. 'And I nearly bumped into those centaurs again. I had to hide up a tree for ages.'

Now that Peleus wasn't boasting, Demon felt a bit sorry for him. Then he had an idea.

'If you help me look for a cure for my griffin,

I'll get all the animals and birds on the mountain to keep an eye out for your sword,' he said. 'I don't know why I didn't think of it before.'

'It's a deal,' said Peleus, clapping Demon so hard on the back that he nearly fell over.

It was so much easier with two people. Peleus wasn't just a boastful warrior. He actually had a brain. The breakthrough came when the prince had the brilliant idea of combining an itching remedy with one for spots. Soon Demon was pounding some sticky white clay with the slimy aloe leaves that grew all over the mountain, a sprinkle of oatmeal and some dried peppermint. Peppermint seemed to cure almost everything.

'How about some of this?' Peleus suggested, holding out a stone jar he'd taken from Chiron's small, tidy kitchen. Demon took a sniff and choked.

'What's THAT?' he spluttered.

'Spiced apple vinegar. My mum swears by it for bug bites, so it might work for spots.'

Demon slopped some in and stirred it about, then looked at the mixture doubtfully. It had turned out like white porridge, and it smelled funny. Never mind, it would have to do. He scraped it into a clay jar and sealed it with a bit of waxed parchment and string. He'd get Chiron to check it when he returned.

'Right,' said Peleus. 'Now where are these animals of yours, young Pandemonius?'

By the time the sun was midway up the sky, Demon had talked to nearly every rabbit, vole, mouse and hare on the mountain. He'd chatted to lynxes, eagles and hawks as well as sparrows, doves and pigeons. None of them had seen a sword, but they'd all promised to spread the word. He was sitting on a rock chatting to a crow when the wolves turned up. Peleus edged behind him.

'Greetings, Pandemonius,' the lead wolf said, as he and his pack settled in a circle at Demon's feet. Wolves were always rather formal, so he bowed his head.

'Greetings, Father Wolf,' he replied. 'Do you bring me news of the prince's sword?'

The wolf's tail wagged, and his jaws lolled open in a sharp-toothed grin.

'Indeed I do,' he said. 'Come forth, Little Stinktail, and tell the son of Pan your story.'

4
LITTLE STINKTAIL

A very small female wolf limped forward from the back of the pack. Her fur might once have been white, but now it was covered in smears of brown, and she definitely deserved her name. Demon coughed and tried not to hold his nose. He could hear Peleus choking behind him.

'I was having a nice roll in a pool of lovely soft cow poo, when something bit me,' she whined. 'It smelled like old rust and blood, and it was like a big, sharp, pointy tooth. It nearly sliced off my paw.' She held up her front paw, which had a deep cut across the pads. 'See?'

'Oh dear,' said Demon. 'That looks bad. I'd better clean it up and put a bandage on it for you.' He looked at Father Wolf. 'Would you be prepared to take my friend to where Little Stinktail was wounded?' he asked.

'Most certainly,' said Father Wolf. 'If he's prepared to run with us, that is.' The big animal looked at Peleus, who was still lurking behind Demon, and licked his chops.

'Is it thinking of eating me?' Peleus whispered, his voice shaking a little. Unlike Demon, he couldn't understand what Father Wolf or Little Stinktail were saying.

Demon laughed. The young warrior wasn't so brave now. 'Of course not,' he said. 'Wolves have a great sense of humour. He reckons it's funny to make you nervous. I think they've found your sword, though, so go with them.'

Once Peleus had jogged off behind the pack,

Demon turned to Little Stinktail and grabbed her by the scruff of the neck.

'You,' he said grimly, 'are coming with me to the waterfall to get scrubbed.'

'What about my poor paw?' Little Stinktail whined. 'You promised me a bandage.'

'Wash first, paw after,' Demon said. 'You don't want cow poo in your wound – it'll make it go all bad.'

The glade by the waterfall was peaceful, and the sun shone through the trees, dappling the grass with spots of greeny gold. By the time Demon had hauled the young wolf into the pool and scrubbed her thoroughly with handfuls of leaves, both of them were soaked through and panting.

'Ugh!' he said, as he inspected her sore paw. 'Now I smell of wet wolf.'

'You've washed off all my nice stinky bits,' she growled, giving him a little nip and shaking herself so that drops of water flew everywhere, catching the sunlight like tiny round rainbows. Demon frowned.

'None of that,' he said. 'I'm only trying to help. We'll have to go back to Chiron's cave.' He tapped the cut pad gently. 'This needs a stitch or two, before the bandage.'

But just as they were leaving, someone trotted through the trees towards them. Someone with thick, hairy goaty legs and big curly horns. Someone with yellow eyes with black, slitty pupils. Someone who wore no clothes and carried a set of silver reed pipes.

Demon dropped to his knees and bowed his head.

'D-Dad! I mean, Your Goddishness,' he said, trying not to let his voice shake. It was still hard to know what to call a father who was also a god. The wolf dropped to her belly and wriggled forward to Pan's feet, wagging her bedraggled tail frantically.

'Hello, son,' said Pan, bending down to stroke Little Stinktail before sweeping Demon up into his arms for a hug. As usual, he smelled of green things and old blood, and his voice was like mossy velvet caught on crumbly bark. 'Got anything for a headache, have you? I've been partying all night with some centaur lads and I might have had a bit too much of Dionysus's new brew.' He put Demon down and rubbed a hand through his wild hair. 'Lethal stuff. Take some advice from your old dad – never touch it, however good it smells.' Pan sank down on a tree stump, groaning a little. The wolf curled up at his hooves, licking at her paw.

Demon looked at his dad. He was a bit paler than normal. What on Zeus's earth did you give a god for a headache though? He looked around him, thinking hard, then he saw the willow tree hanging over the pool.

'I've got just the thing,' he said, taking out a small, sharp knife from his belt. Whispering thanks to the tree, he shaved off a few thin strips of bark, shredded them and held them out. 'Chew these,' he said. 'They'll be bitter, but it'll take the pain away.'

After making disgusted faces for a few minutes, Pan spat out the chewed bark and sat up, looking a lot brighter.

'Clever lad,' he said. 'You'll be as great a healer as Chiron in no time.' Demon glowed with pride. Praise from his father meant a lot to him, and he didn't often get it. He didn't often see him, in fact.

Pan stretched, the great muscles in his chest rippling. 'I must be off again,' he said. 'But before I go, is there anything I can give you, son?'

Demon knew he should probably say 'nothing', but this was too good a chance to pass up.

'Is there a way I can use your pipes to put just one animal to sleep at a time?' he asked, trying to keep the eagerness out of his voice. A look of pleased surprise crossed Pan's face.

'What? No magic cloak of invisibility or sandals with wings?' he asked. 'Not that I'm very good at those, but it's usually what people ask for.' Demon shook his head.

'I'm sure they'd be nice, but I'd rather learn to use your pipes properly,' he said. 'They've been very useful so far.'

'Very well then, my boy.' The forest god raised his pipes to his lips. 'Look into the beast's eyes, and

46

do this.' He blew a tricky little low twiddle, which raised all the hairs on the back of Demon's neck. Then he played a high, screechy set of notes which made Demon's teeth hurt. 'That's the wake-up one as well in case you need it. Now you try them.'

After Pan had left, Demon practised all the way back to Chiron's cave until he had the notes just right. Then he looked into Little Stinktail's eyes and put her to sleep while he sewed and bandaged her paw. By the time he'd woken her up again, Chiron was back.

Demon showed him the ointment he and Peleus had made. As the centaur sniffed it, and gave Demon an approving nod, Demon thought of something.

'How do I get Arnie's feathers to grow back?' he asked. 'There are too many of them to stick on, and anyway, I don't think I've got any of the glue left from when Autolycus stole the pegasi feathers.'

Chiron looked at him. 'I don't approve of that box of yours normally, but didn't I hear something about you regrowing the feathers on some Stymphalian Birds a while back? You could add a few drops of that medicine to the ointment if you've got any left. Otherwise, I'm afraid it's time and patience.' He handed Demon a mask, a bag of pungent herbs and a huge bottle of green liquid. 'Burn all the straw from the griffin's cage, then fumigate the stables with this sage. Tomorrow at dawn, you must sprinkle the whole place with my patent cleaning liquid. When Eos awakes is when the ingredients are at their strongest. Don't forget now. It's important.'

As Demon got off the Iris Express, his head was buzzing with his teacher's instructions. He ran straight to the hospital shed, and found the small phial of feather regrowth medicine. Luckily, there were a few drops left. Mixing them into Arnie's ointment with a spoon, he walked over to see the griffin.

Arnie was not in a good mood. The griffin was stalking around the cage, growling and emitting ear-piercingly angry shrieks. The purple spots were now huge and glowing, and some of the ones on its head had burst in showers of revolting yellow pus, which oozed and trickled down its beak.

'YUCK!' said Demon, before he could stop himself. 'That's disgusting.'

As he put down the ointment and let himself into the cage, Arnie's beak whipped out quicker than a bolt of lightning and snapped off Demon's left little finger, spitting it out immediately.

'I warned you, Pan's scrawny kid! I warned you!' it screamed.

Demon screamed too. He couldn't help it. The little stump was pouring with blood, but there was no time to fix it, because Arnie was coming at him again, this time going for his bare toes.

Frantically, Demon grabbed his pipes with his right hand, looked into Arnie's eyes, and blew Pan's new twiddle. Immediately the griffin dropped like a dead thing, slumped on his back with outspread wings and head lolling to the side. Trying not to scream again, Demon fell to his knees, searching for his finger. Was it too late? Had it been burned up by toxic griffin spit? No, there it was!

'Offy! Yukus!' he gasped, holding up the bit of his finger. It looked like a limp pink slug. 'Help!' The healing snakes whipped into action, one taking the finger in its tail and pressing it to the stump, the other squirting golden liquid onto the join from its fangs. Demon began to see stars, silver and green and purple, floating in front of his eyes. Then everything went black.

He woke to find himself sprawled beside a sleeping Arnie, with a snake tongue tickling each earlobe.

'Whaa–?' he murmured, as his eyes focused again. He looked at his hand. It was a bit smeary with blood, but his little finger was back as if it had never gone. 'Oh, thank goodness,' he said. 'I'd be lost without you two. What a good thing I didn't say anything to Chiron after all.'

'A pleasssure asss alwaysss, young massster,' the snakes hissed.

Demon scrambled up and went to the hospital

shed to wash. Then he came back to the griffin's pen and smeared all Arnie's feathered bits with the new ointment. By the time he'd done his chores and followed Chiron's instructions, including making a bonfire of the straw in Arnie's old pen, his eyes were closing on their own. He fell into bed, needing desperately to sleep, but every time he dropped off, he jerked awake from horrible dreams about sharp griffin beaks and missing fingers, then worried that another of his feathered beasts might have caught the Purple Spotted Feather Plague.

5

OWL EMERGENCY

Dawn came far too soon. As Eos drew back her pink curtains Demon sprang out of bed, seizing the huge bottle of green liquid. He went round every pen, sprinkling all the beasts and every inch of the stables as he mucked out. The Caucasian Eagle was not at all keen on being sprinkled, nor on being sent away to spend time with Prometheus.

'I have to peck his disgusting liver out every day – I don't need to socialise with the guy too,' it grumbled, giving Demon a sharp peck. 'He keeps asking me to go and talk to Zeus's eagle for him. As if I'm some kind of best mates with that scary old bird.' It flapped off eventually, still grumbling, but promising not to come back till Demon sent word.

The pegasi were not too keen on the green liquid either.

'It smells of rotten grass,' they whinnied, rearing and bucking and battering him with their wings till Demon had to duck and dodge for fear of being trampled. He sniffed at it. It did stink a bit underneath – but it also smelled of nice things like eucalyptus, ginger, hyssop, lavender and thyme.

'Do you really want all your feathers to drop out, and your skin to break out in purple popping spots?' he asked Keith, the boss pegasus, after the herd had calmed down a bit. Keith rubbed his tiny gold horns against Demon's shoulder.

'Nohohoho,' he neighed, just as Demon heard a very strange noise indeed outside the stables.

Hic-a-hoot, hic-a-hoot, hic-a-hoot.

He put down his bottle and went to investigate. As he saw the tall figure in silver armour approaching, his heart started to thump so hard that he could almost feel it trying to burst out through his ribs. Athena, Goddess of Wisdom, had come to visit, and in his experience, a visit from one of the Olympian gods or goddesses was never good news. Normally it led to threats of leg-mincing or seabed-scrubbing or plain old burnt-to-a-little-pile-of-charcoal-ing.

'Oh do get up, Pandemonius,' she said, as he dropped to his knees in the dust. 'There's no time for that. My poor Sophie here has got a terrible case of the upside-down hiccups. She just can't seem to stop.' Athena made a face. 'She keeps cuddling up and giving me horrible, smelly owl kisses too.' As she spoke, the enormous owl on Athena's rather stained-looking shoulder snuggled in under the goddess's silver helmet and nibbled on her ear lovingly, continuing to *hic-a-hoot* as she did so. Suddenly, there was a particularly loud hiccup, and out of her beak shot a stream of mangled mouse bones and other more unmentionable things. Demon dodged one particularly juicy something that splatted on the ground at his feet with a wet squelch. *Oh no!* he thought. *Just what I don't need – another sick feathered creature!* What should he do? He had to warn Athena about the Purple Spotted Feather Plague, even if it made her angry.

He cleared his throat, with a high, squeaking sound like a mouse whose tail has just been stepped on.

'P-Please don't bring her any closer, Your Wondrous Wiseness,' he said, holding up a hand. 'I don't want her to catch the Purple Spotted Feather Plague as well as the hiccups.'

Athena stepped back hurriedly. 'Explain, stable boy,' she said, in the kind of voice that would have frozen any nearby volcanoes. 'Fast.' She pointed her silver spear at him menacingly, its sharp tip levelled right at his thumping heart.

So Demon explained, almost tripping over his words in an effort not to be stabbed.

'Very well then,' said Athena when he'd finished. 'I shall leave Sophie roosting in one of my olive trees by the Iris Express. She'll be safe there, and then you can take her down to Chiron with the pegasi.' She stroked the owl's soft feathers, looking worried, then frowned at Demon, her grey eyes flashing silver sparks. 'You'd better have her cured by this afternoon, or I shall turn you into a nice fat black olive and crush you into oil,' she said, turning to leave. 'I've got to go and sort out an argument between Eos and Tithonus now, but I'll be down to collect her later. Don't mess this up, Pandemonius. I've got a meeting with Zeus after that, and he won't appreciate it if that big eagle of his catches whatever Sophie's got. Or the Purple Spotted Feather Plague, for that matter.'

As the goddess left, Demon let out a sigh of relief so huge that it almost blew down the door of the stables. That silver spear of Athena's had come so close to his heart, he'd almost felt it. But he couldn't think about that – or about being squished and squashed into olive oil – he had too much else to do.

'Arnie,' he muttered. 'Must see to Arnie.' He trotted over to the isolation pen, and put a very cautious eye to the bars. The griffin was still lying exactly where Demon had left it the night before, on its back. Loud, scratchy snores were coming from its beak, and its eyes were firmly closed.

'Arnie?' Demon whispered. 'Arnie? Are you awake?' But there was no reply. The new pipe twiddle he'd learned from his dad was still working. He let himself into the pen and inspected the purple spots. They had definitely receded, though there were still a few left. Demon bent closer. Was that a new feather he saw? Yes! A row of new, tiny feathers had appeared right on top of Arnie's head. The ointment must be taking effect!

Demon reached for the now half-empty pot and started to smear on another layer. There was no harm in putting on a little extra, just in case. Unfortunately, one of the bigger spots on Arnie's neck burst with a loud *POP!* just as he touched it, leaking horrid yellow slime onto his hand and all over his chiton.

'YUCK!' he said, jumping back and grabbing a handful of straw to wipe it off with. 'I can see I'm going to be washing a LOT if this carries on.'

Demon knew that when he eventually woke Arnie up, he'd be crankier than a cross manticore and hungrier than at least fifty packs of starving hellhounds. He'd need to find more than ambrosia cake if the griffin wasn't to chomp on all his other fingers and toes – and probably the rest of him as well.

As he shut the pen and went to scrub and change, he scratched his head absentmindedly, thinking. Maybe one of the kitchen fauns would help. But he'd have to find something to bribe it with. What did fauns like? Shells? He had some of those from his time down in Poseidon's watery kingdom. Or maybe he'd have to give up his spider-silk blanket . . .

Demon thought all the way to the kitchens, but he still hadn't come up with a suitable bribe by the time he got there. As usual, it was a riot of heat and good smells. His mouth watered as the scent of his favourite honey cakes reached his nose. Surely he could beg for just one?

A large hand fell on his shoulder, and he leapt into the air, letting out a squeal of fright.

'What are you doing, sneaking round my kitchen, Pandemonius?' asked a voice like cream and honey on hot rocks. Oh no! He'd been caught by Hestia, Goddess of the Hearth and creator of all things delicious. She gave him a little shake. 'Don't bother trying to lie to me, young stable boy, because I'll know.' She took him by one ear and turned him round to face her.

'It's Arnie,' Demon began. The story poured out of him for the second time that day. 'And . . . and the griffin says it needs a special diet of minced lamb with blood gravy and a sprinkle of scarab beetles to get better,' Demon finished.

Hestia frowned, tapping the silver ladle she held against her hip.

'And what will you give me if I make the beast what it asks for?' she said. If thinking of something for a faun had been hard, thinking of something for a goddess was practically impossible. Demon didn't even try.

'What do you need, Your Goddessness?' he asked, trembling a little. 'I'll give you anything.'

She smiled. It was a smile with teeth in it.

'Don't make rash promises to goddesses, Pandemonius. They can lead you into all sorts of trouble. Just tell my brother the centaur that I need a bunch of five-leaved panax and a pot of bee gold from his stores. Bring it with you when you return to Olympus. When I have them in my hands I will make your beast its food — though I do draw the line at sprinkled scarabs.' She ruffled his hair. 'I have a soft spot for you, young stable boy — heavens know why!'

Demon looked up at her.

'Th-thank you, Your Amazingness,' he stammered. He had no idea what five-leaved panax or bee gold were, but he could find out.

'Well, that's settled then,' said Hestia, towing him into the kitchen behind her like a small bobbing toy behind a very large boat. 'Now, come and taste my new batch of honey cakes.'

6
ATHENA'S TERRIBLE TASK

By the time Demon had licked the last of the honey cake from around his mouth, it was time to load the pegasi and Sophie the owl onto the Iris Express. The pegasi were very overexcited about their holiday, and kept leaping into the air and doing little loop-the-loop somersaults. As soon as Sophie saw him coming, she flapped out of her olive tree and onto his shoulder, wrapping one wing round his head and nibbling his ear lovingly between hiccups. Demon peered round at her.

'Have you stopped spewing out mouse bones and stuff?' he asked. 'Only this is my last clean chiton.' Sophie just let out a mournful *hic-a-hoot* and snuggled in closer.

The Iris Express arrived in a flash of rainbow light, and soon Demon was busy trying to herd all the pegasi aboard.

'Go!' he shouted, as the last hoof and tail crowded in. Demon tried not to look down. He was very near the edge, and there wasn't much room. Suddenly a familiar stench hit his nostrils.

'Oh no!' he said, as he looked down. Golden balls of pegasi poo were rolling around on the floor at his feet. 'Who was that?' he asked sternly. The sturdy palomino mare called Sky Pearl hung her head.

'Meheeheehee,' she neighed.

'Well, try not to, the rest of you,' Demon said sternly. 'Iris won't like it.'

'Indeed I will not,' said Iris. Transparent rainbow arms picked up Sky Pearl under her wings and dangled her outside the rainbow. 'If you do it again, I'll drop all of you into the sea. See how you like THAT!'

After that, the journey was not the smooth, swift ride Demon was used to. Iris bumped and jolted her passengers all the way down to Chiron's cave, and spilled them out onto the grass in a heap. She left in a huff, snarling.

'Go and graze, you lot,' Demon said. 'And don't let them fly off, Keith.'

'I wohohohon't,' Keith whinnied, putting his head down and tearing at the long, green grass.

'Now,' said Demon, 'let's see if we can find some owl medicine.'

But just as he spoke, Sophie fell off his shoulder, flapping madly. She lay on the ground, eyes spinning like kaleidoscopes. An enormous *hic-a-hoot* erupted from her beak, and with it, a transparent pink heart-shaped bubble, followed by lots of smaller ones. Demon picked her up and stood her upright.

'What in the name of Athena's eyebrows is wrong with that owl?' asked a soft voice. Demon spun round. Standing astride two jagged rocks on the mountainside above was a tall nymph, dressed in floaty greys and greens and browns which made her look like a part of the stones themselves. She jumped down to join Peleus, who had come out of the cave, a great big smile on his face. He was brandishing a shiny silver sword, which flashed shards of sunlight into Demon's eyes, making him blink.

'Look, Pandemonius!' he said. 'The wolves found it for me! Thank you ever so much – I owe you a massive favour. Whatever you want, really, just ask!'

Demon's eyebrows shot right up into his curly hair. Was this the arrogant young man he'd met only yesterday? Had finding the magic sword really made Chiron's grandson into this happy, smiling person? Then Peleus put an arm round the tall nymph, hugging her tightly.

'This is my mum, Endeis, by the way. She's the oread of this mountain.'

'You have my gratitude too, Pandemonius,' said

Endeis, in a joyful, bubbly voice that sounded like a waterfall tumbling through sunlight. 'You did a very brave thing saving my son from those centaurs. But we can talk about that later. Right now your owl definitely has a problem that needs fixing.'

Demon wasn't going to disagree. Sophie was *hic-a-hoot*-ing so fast that the pink heart bubbles had formed a thick cloud around both of them. Quickly, he picked her up and ran into the cave. Surely there must be something about curing hiccups in one of Chiron's books. Although he'd never heard of anyone hiccupping out pink hearts.

'What have you eaten, Sophie?' he asked. But the owl couldn't answer. She was too busy hiccupping and trying to give Demon more owl kisses.

'Stop it,' Demon said, fending her off. 'If you can't speak, then you'll have to flap. Once for yes, twice for no, all right?'

Sophie flapped once.

'Did you eat anything you wouldn't normally eat?'

Flap.

'Did someone give it to you?'

Flap, flap.

Endeis interrupted.

'Did you steal it from one of the gods?' she asked. Demon didn't know that nymphs could speak owl. He'd thought he was the only one who could, apart from his dad.

Sophie's eyes started to spin the other way, and she hiccupped out a very small heart.

Flap.

All at once Demon remembered something Hephaestus had said.

'Have you been anywhere near Eros?' he asked. 'Did you swallow something with a love potion in it?

Flap.

'Right,' said Demon. 'That's it! I've seen a love potion antidote somewhere. Chiron had to make one up the other day for some poor girl who'd fallen in love with a tree.'

Peleus laughed.

'A tree? Are you serious?'

'Deadly serious,' said Demon, searching along the shelves. 'She made little garlands for its branches and everything. Said she wanted to marry it. That was one of Eros's potions too. He said it was a joke.' He closed his lips tightly in case he said something he shouldn't. Even if Eros was a god, he shouldn't play tricks like that. It wasn't very kind.

'Is this it?' asked Endeis, holding up a clear bottle of bright blue potion.

'Yes!' said Demon, 'Quick! Pass it here!'

It took five drops of potion for Sophie's eyes to go back to normal, and for the pink hearts to stop. She was just explaining how she'd eaten some tasty sugar mice she'd found in Eros's room when Athena arrived. Her eyes were wild and her silver helmet was all askew. Sophie flew straight to her shoulder, but the goddess was so distracted that she didn't even seem to notice that her owl was cured.

'Where's Chiron?' she asked Demon. 'I need him. Immediately.'

'I'm afraid he doesn't seem to be here, Your Wiseness.'

'Well, go and fetch him at once. Run, boy! Run! It's an emergency!' Demon looked round at Peleus and Endeis frantically – he had no idea where his teacher had gone, nor any clue where to look.

'It's no use Pandemonius running anywhere,' Endeis said. 'My father's gone off to tend Asclepius's baby. There were complications with the birth. He left a message with me. He won't be back for at least a week, and he's not to be disturbed.'

Athena stamped her foot. A small crack appeared in the mountainside and the ground shook. Endeis took a step forward.

'Mind my mountain,' she said crossly. 'You'll break it.'

Athena turned on her and roared. Silver sparks shot out of her eyes, skittering across the ground where they fell, making the grass curl and shrivel.

'Blasted nymph,' she shouted. 'Your stupid father is NEVER where he's supposed to be. Who's going to cure that wretched phoenix now?' Her sparking eyes fell on Demon.

'You! Pandemonius! You'll have to do it.'

'M-m-me?'

'Yes, you! You're supposed to be a healer, aren't you? Surely a phoenix can't be much harder to fix than an owl. The beastly bird has gone blind and lost its voice just when it needs to build its nest. I got a fire message from Antaeus, its guardian.' She stamped her foot again, and another jagged trench opened up at Demon's feet. 'Why now?' the goddess yelled, flinging her helmet on the ground and stamping on it. 'Just when Zeus has commanded me to help some wretched hero son of his kill a gorgon.' Her eyes fell on Demon again and she flapped a hand at him, emitting a shower of stinging silver darts. 'Go!' she said. 'Why are you still here?'

'I-I don't know where to go, Your Knowledgeableness,' he said, feeling his stomach drop into his toes as he dodged her silver missiles, rather unsuccessfully. They pierced his skin, burning like the stings of a thousand wasps. Was this it? Was this finally going to be where he was turned into a pile of smoking cinders?

Athena tutted impatiently.

'Do you know nothing? The phoenix lives in a cave at the top of the Mountains of Burning Sand, right in the middle of a desert. The Iris Express knows where.' She glared at him. 'If the phoenix isn't able to sing its Song of Renewal at the right moment, then the fire devils it guards will escape and steal all its power. Do you know what that means, stable boy?'

Demon shook his head, picking darts out of his ears.

'You like birds and beasts, don't you, Pandemonius?'

He nodded as Athena bent towards him.

'If the fire devils are let loose on the world, they will burn up the nearby forest where millions of the most wonderful creatures on earth live. Every death will give the fire devils more power – and then they will turn on US!' She hissed like a striking snake and lifted him up by the front of his chiton till their noses were nearly touching.

'So if you don't cure that bird, so that it can sing its Song of Renewal, YOU will be responsible for the deaths of all those beasts – and maybe even the safety of Olympus itself!' Her voice dropped to a low growl. 'Don't fail me, Pandemonius. Or I will ask Father Zeus to take care of you personally. And I don't mean with ambrosia and honey cakes.'

With that, the goddess shot up into the air faster than a streak of silver lightning and disappeared, a wavering hoot of farewell from Sophie lingering on the air.

'Oh no!' Demon whispered, sinking to his knees as he picked slivers of silver out of his shoulder and chest. It was his most impossible task yet.

7

MIGHTY ANTAEUS

'No time for that, said Endeis, hauling him to his feet. 'Pack what you need while I call the Iris Express for you.'

As he rushed into the cave, Demon's thoughts whirled madly, like snowflakes in a blizzard. What would he need?

'Eyebright and chamomile for blindness, slippery elm and marshmallow for sore throats, aloe for burns,' he panted, throwing bandages, bowls, cloths and everything else he could think of into one of Chiron's herb-gathering sacks.

'And this,' said Peleus, holding out Chiron's own personal big *Book of Cures*. The one that was chained to the wall. The one he was forbidden to touch.

'I can't take that,' said Demon. 'Chiron said it must never leave the cave.'

'Well, he's not here. And it's an emergency,' said Peleus, unhooking it. So Demon stowed it in the sack, along with his opticles. Was that everything?

'Oh no!' he groaned. 'My Pyro-Protection Suit! It's back on Olympus. I'll have to go and get it. I'll get burnt up by those fire devils otherwise.' He rushed outside, only to see the Iris Express disappearing into the sky.

'Nooo! Iris,' he called. 'Come back! Please! I need you!' But there was no answer, only the splatting sound of a pile of liquid pegasi poo falling at his feet.

'She's gone on strike,' Endeis said. 'Said she's

never carrying you again till you apologise at least three times on your bended knees and scrub her inside out twenty times till she's shiny again. Some of those pegasi had another poo accident before they landed, apparently. Rather a runny one, as you can see.'

Demon's whole body felt hollow, as if his skin was going to collapse. Prickles of cold ran all over him. There was no chance of getting his Pyro-Protection Suit or anything else from Olympus now. And then a worse thought occurred to him.

'What am I going to do?' he whispered. 'However am I going to get to the Mountains of Burning Sand? The phoenix won't be able to sing, the fire devils will escape, and all those wonderful creatures will be burnt up.' He gulped. 'And what if they burn up the gods and goddesses too? What will happen to us all?' He didn't want to think about that – or about Father Zeus himself coming after him. He wouldn't even be a pile of charcoal if that happened. He'd be nothing at all.

'Mountains of Burning Sahahahand?' neighed

Keith, flying over the jagged trench that now cut off access to the cave. 'Thahahat's near our earthly home.' Demon turned to him eagerly.

'Do you know the way there, Keith? Could you take me?'

The little boss pegasus swished his black tail.

'Maybe,' he whinnied. 'If I get a LOT of itchy-scratches.'

'I'll give you as many itchy-scratches as you want,' Demon said, flinging his arms round Keith's neck. 'How far is it? Can we get there quickly?'

Keith shook his head, his mane flying into Demon's eyes. 'It's a long wayheyhey,' he snorted.

Demon groaned. He needed to get there fast – Athena had said it was an emergency. And how could he leave his beasts again – what about Arnie? Would he really stay asleep till Demon got back? But as usual, he knew he didn't have a choice. Curing the phoenix was more important than anything.

'Who's going to look after the stables?' Demon said. He couldn't ignore his responsibilities. 'If they begin to smell of poo again, I'll have the goddesses after me as well as Zeus. Doris can't be trusted on her own – and Arnie's no more use than a broken chariot wheel right now.'

'I'll do it,' said Endeis. 'I can visit my nymph and dryad friends at the same time. I haven't seen Althea for ages. I've been too busy being queen and taking care of things back at the palace on Aegina.' She frowned. 'And of Peleus's dad, of course. It'll do them all good to be without me for a while.'

'I've decided I'm coming with you to the Mountains of Burning Sand,' said Peleus. 'You might need a friend to guard your back. Those fire devils sound dangerous. Anyway, it'll be an adventure.' He grinned, winking at Demon with one bright green eye.

Demon looked at Peleus doubtfully. He was quite tall.

'I'm not sure you'll fit on a pegasus,' he said.

'I'll carry him,' said Sky Pearl, trotting forward. 'I'm strong.'

Quickly Demon and Peleus loaded up the medicine sack and another bag full of food and several waterskins. They also found some ropes, which they tied round themselves and the little horses.

'Just in case we fall asleep or need to haul each other up the mountain,' Peleus said, slinging his sword across his back and climbing onto Sky Pearl. He did look a bit funny, with his long legs dangling nearly to the ground, but Demon didn't feel much like laughing. He had a blind, voiceless phoenix to cure – and he hadn't a clue how to do it.

They flew and flew until the bones in their bottoms ached from sitting, over land, over sea, and then over land again. As Helios and his chariot rolled through the sky above them, Demon waved to his friend Abraxas and the other celestial horses. Soon it was night. The stars shone cold and distant, like diamonds on deep blue velvet. Demon tried to count them to pass the time, but all too quickly he felt his eyelids drooping.

'Ooh,' he said, wriggling. 'However am I going to keep awake and not fall off?' He clutched at Keith's mane, winding it round and round his wrists.

'Ouchy!' Keith whinnied. 'Don't hold on so hard! And stop wiggling about!'

'Lucky we tied ourselves on!' Peleus called over. 'I'm sleepy too.'

'Tell us about the Mountains of Burning Sand, Keith,' said Demon. 'And about whatsisname? Antaeus? Maybe that'll keep us from falling asleep.'

'Antacus is a mighty giant,' Keith whinnied. 'Big as a mountain. We don't go near him. He has a nasty club. He likes to fight.'

Naturally, Athena hadn't bothered to say anything about a giant, Demon thought. That was so typical of the gods – they never thought you needed to know things like that.

'That sounds scary,' he said, shivering. He'd never met a giant – and he wasn't sure he wanted to.

'Is scary,' neighed Sky Pearl. 'Smells bad too. Like dead people.'

'I knew you'd need me, Demon,' said Peleus cheerfully. 'I'll fight him. I've fought LOTS of people with my magic sword. I never lose. Well, almost never,' he added.

'But he's a GIANT!' Demon said.

'So?' said Peleus boastfully. 'My sword is sharp, and I fear nothing and nobody.' Demon thought about how nervous Peleus had looked around the wolves, but wisely chose not to mention it.

As they flew into the dawn of another day, Demon began to smell a spicy green scent wafting up from below. Eos's pink light started to fill the east, and he saw a vast expanse of forest below them.

'Is that the place Athena talked about?' he asked. 'The one with all the amazing creatures in it?'

'Yes,' Keith neighed. 'Look! There's a herd of tallnecks! See? In the glade.'

Demon peered down. The most extraordinary animals he'd ever seen were grazing the treetops. They had long necks that allowed them to reach the topmost branches, and tiny horns shaped like a snail's. They were spotty and dappled, like shade, and their backs sloped downwards so that their legs were shorter at the back than the front. Demon longed to ask Keith to land so he could talk to them, but he knew he mustn't. Instead he must save the phoenix so that these marvellous creatures weren't all burnt up.

'How far to go?' he asked, wishing that Keith's poor little wings could flap even faster.

'Still far,' Keith whinnied. 'But you can see the mountains now — and the desert.' In the distance, golden peaks caught the first rays from Helios, turning them to a blaze of red flame. As they flew through the day, the mountains grew bigger and bigger till they dwarfed everything around them.

As dusk fell, Demon could see a tiny figure leaping and running across the sand towards the forest.

'I wonder who that is?' he said. But there was no time to find out.

'Going down!' Sky Pearl and Keith called as they dipped their wings, gliding towards a flat piece of land outside a cave in the rocks. It was covered in a carpet of tiny golden flowers, which gave off a scent like honey, just by a stone well with a bucket beside it.

'Sand flowers!' Sky Pearl whinnied, tipping Peleus off unceremoniously and burying her nose in the fragrant blossoms.

'Yummy-scrum!' Keith skidded to a halt beside her, his wings drooping.

'Itchy-scratch?' he asked hopefully, as Demon clambered off, legs as limp as jellied sand snakes. Demon gave the boss pegasus's ears a good scratching as Keith too buried his nose in the flowers and started munching.

'Hey!' Peleus shouted from the direction of the cave. 'Come over here! I don't think I'm going to have to fight the giant after all – someone's already done it!'

Demon grabbed his healing sack and stumbled over to the dark entrance. Sticking out of it were two thick, hairy legs, with rusty iron greaves buckled round them. As Demon clambered past, he saw Peleus squatting beside an enormous head. The giant Antaeus was almost as broad as he was tall, with more iron armour strapped to his arms and chest. The vast, sausage-like fingers on his left hand lay limp around a huge spiked club, hung with chains. About his shoulders hung a hooded cloak of shimmering feathers, which shone and shifted like fire, lighting up the rest of the cave.

Demon's breath caught in his throat as the blank, black eyes of a thousand skulls looked down at him. At least they weren't alive, like the ones he'd met in Hades' underworld kingdom, he hastily assured himself before looking away quickly.

'Is he breathing?' Demon asked anxiously. There was no time to be scared.

'I think so,' said Peleus. 'Someone's given him a big whack on the head, though. Look!' Lifting the giant's short, red hair, he pointed to a big purple lump on his already knobbly forehead.

Demon shook the gigantic shoulder.

'Antaeus! Antaeus! Wake up!'

8

HORRIBLE HERACLES STRIKES AGAIN

'Nyaarrghh!' shouted the giant in a great, rumbling voice, sitting up so suddenly that he knocked Peleus head over heels. 'Whassermatter?' He looked round wildly. 'Where is he? Where's that Heracles? Let me at him?' Then, quite suddenly, his eyes rolled back in his head and he slumped to the ground again, quite unconscious.

Demon jumped up, fists clenched. An angry ball of rage flared up inside his belly as he glared round the cave. Horrible Heracles? Was he still here? Demon eyed Antaeus's club. Would he be strong enough to lift it? He owed Heracles a few good whacks for being so nasty to the poor beasts in the stables. And now he'd knocked out the very person Demon needed most! Then Demon remembered the tiny running figure he'd seen as they'd flown over the desert.

'Bother!' he said. It was no use. The beast-bashing hero would be far away by now. 'I'll get you one day, Horrible Heracles,' he muttered.

Sighing, he shook the giant's armour-clad shoulder again, but there was no response.

'Burning feathers,' he muttered. 'That's what I need.' Quickly, he pulled a handful of the shining plumes out of Antaeus's cloak and lit them at the tiny covered fire that burned at the back of the cave.

Immediately there was a smell of singed cinnamon and spice mixed with something that caught at the back of his throat and made him cough. Demon blew the flame out and waved the smoking feathers under Antaeus's nose.

'Gaarrgh!' the giant exclaimed, sitting up again. 'What is that disgusting smell?' He fanned one of his plate-sized hands in front of his face. Then he howled, clutching at his chest. 'Ow! My ribs!'

'Are you properly awake now?' Demon asked, stepping back to a safe distance. He still didn't know how friendly Antaeus was. 'Athena got your message. She's sent me to heal the phoenix. Can you take us to it?'

'Phoenix?' Antaeus asked, rubbing his head in a confused way. 'What phoenix? I don't know what you're talking about.' He looked round. 'Where's that pesky Heracles gone? I need his skull for my collection!' He blinked sleepily. 'And who are you two, my little shrimps? You're not big enough or ugly enough to be heroes.'

'I'm Prince Peleus, he's Pandemonius, and never mind about Heracles,' Peleus said impatiently. 'The phoenix is what's important now. You know – the one you're supposed to be guarding? The one that's gone blind and has no voice?'

'Still not with you,' said the giant, picking his nose and inspecting the slimy green result before popping it in his mouth.

'It's that bump. He's had all the sense knocked out of him by Horrible Heracles,' said Demon, pulling ointment and bandages out of his sack. 'Quick! Go and get him some water from the well. That might help his memory.'

'You get it,' said Peleus sulkily. 'I'm a prince, not your servant.' Then he saw the fierce look in Demon's eye. 'Oh, all right,' he grumbled. 'I'll give the pegasi some first, though. They must be thirsty after flying us all this way.'

Demon immediately felt bad. He should have thought of that. Quickly, he smeared bruise-flower ointment on the bump and rolled bandages round Antaeus's ribs under the armour. It was really hard and fiddly, even though his hands were small. The giant groaned throughout, and wriggled about. He was being much more difficult than any of Demon's beast patients.

'Don't be such a baby,' Demon said, just as

Peleus came back, puffing and slopping water everywhere.

'This stuff tastes amazing,' he said. 'Like liquid sunlight.' It was true. The water in the bucket glowed slightly.

'Maybe it'll help,' said Demon hopefully. He dipped a clay cup full and put it to the giant's lips. Antaeus slurped it down, dribbling it disgustingly down his front.

'More,' he said. After sixteen further cups, he burped loudly. 'Marvellous stuff,' he said 'My magic well always does the trick.' Then he clapped a hand to his forehead, where the bump had already disappeared. 'The phoenix! I remember now.' He looked round. 'Where's old Chiron, then? The poor creature is in great need. It's got much worse since I sent Athena that message.'

'Athena sent me instead,' said Demon.

Antaeus looked down at him doubtfully.

'Bit small for a healer, aren't you?'

'Never mind my size,' said Demon crossly. 'Do

you want the phoenix fixed or not? Athena said it was pretty urgent.'

'And so it is, shrimp boy,' said Antaeus. 'Come on, then. Up on my shoulders, the both of you. I'll have you there faster than Apollo can fire an arrow.'

'Let's take some of that magic water with us,' said Peleus. 'It might come in handy.'

'Good thinking,' said Antaeus, smiling a smile full of broken brown teeth. 'Helios blessed my well with healing powers long ago. It cures nearly anything. Now why didn't I think of that when the phoenix first got sick? He's a clever lad for a prince, that Peleus, isn't he?' Demon nodded a bit sourly, wishing he'd thought of it himself.

Once the waterskins were full, and Demon had made sure that the pegasi were happy, the giant grabbed Demon in one hand and Peleus in the other, tossing them and the bags into the air and onto his shoulders as if they were straws. The armour wasn't very comfortable to sit on, though the feather cloak gave them a bit of padding. They had to hang on to the giant's ears to avoid being jiggled off as Antaeus bolted up the side of the mountain. His gigantic strides gobbled up the distance faster than a starving siren eats sailors.

As they neared the top, he skidded to a halt outside a rather grand cave. It had crumbling pillars either side of it which were carved with very ancient-looking pictures of flames, strange-looking birds, eggs and suns. That wasn't what caught Demon's eye, though. Covering the whole entrance was a golden cascade, not of water, but of fire, which lit up the night like a torch.

'Through there!' Antaeus said, as Demon and Peleus slid down to the ground, landing with two loud bumps, which raised a cloud of sparkling dust. Demon gaped at him.

'How do we get through *that*?' he asked, pointing at the firefall. Oh *how* he wished he'd brought his Pyro-Protection Suit. 'We'll get all burned up! Isn't there another way through?'

Antaeus shook his head.

'How do you get in, then?' Peleus asked.

'With this, of course,' said Antaeus, pointing to his cloak. 'It's made of phoenix feathers. They're flameproof.' He fumbled in a pocket, pulling out a mask, also made of feathers. 'And I put this on too.'

'You'll have to take us in underneath your cloak, then,' said Demon. 'There's no time to lose.'

'There's not a lot of room,' said Peleus. 'We'll have to go one at a time.'

'Well, I'm going first,' said Demon, grabbing the medicine sack. 'I'm not leaving that poor bird a moment longer than I have to.'

'Brave little shrimp,' said Antaeus, throwing the cloak wide. 'Crawl under, then!'

'Don't call me a shrimp,' Demon said, as Antaeus settled him in the crook of one arm and pulled the cloak tight shut again. But Antaeus just laughed, a great, earthquake rumble that shook Demon right down to his toes.

Demon had never felt heat like it, not even when Hera had nearly frizzled him to a frazzle, or the Bronze Bulls were trying to burn Olympus up.

There was a blinding flash as his feet began to sizzle, and then they were through. Antaeus let Demon down, then went back for Peleus. Demon checked to see that his toes were all still there, then looked around wonderingly.

The cave walls were made of a buttery-smooth white stone, which had soft lights flickering within it, changing from rose to pale green to the exact soft blue of an early morning sky. They went up and up, and where they met the top, crystal stalactites hung down like rainbow daggers, reflecting the lights from below. The floor was shining black, and right in the middle of it sat a massive ruby, bigger than a giant-sized boulder, its centre glowing and pulsing weakly. It looked like a heart in trouble, Demon thought, sniffing as a delightful smell wafted into his nostrils.

Piled up at one side of the gigantic jewel was a messy heap of sweetly scented pieces of wood, some long, some short, mixed higgledy-piggledy with slivers of bark, dried flowers, bright fruits and bunches of various berries. Slumped on top of the ruby was a huge bird. Demon could tell immediately that it was in trouble. Its head lolled over the edge, its long, flowing tail feathers were dull and lifeless, and it was coughing, making a horrible, weak tearing sound, which Demon immediately knew was not a good sign.

'Oh, you poor thing,' he said, running over to it. But the ruby towered over him and, jump as he might, he couldn't get a grip to clamber up its slippery sides.

'Hey!' said Peleus, arriving with Antaeus behind him. 'Look at the fire devils!' He pointed to the back of the cave. In his hurry to reach the phoenix, Demon hadn't even noticed the transparent crystal wall at the rear, half hidden by the bulk of the ruby. Suddenly he felt as if a large fist had slammed into his chest. Behind the crystal were skinny red creatures, capering and shrieking with glee. They had unnaturally long arms and legs, with sharp-taloned hands and feet. Their heads were huge, and their eyes were pits of dark flame. It was the mouths that were the worst, though. They gaped hungrily, showing rows of needle-sharp teeth, and each blew out a jet of blue-white flame, which skittered over the surface of their prison.

'Oh no,' said Demon, his voice trembling. Because at the top of the crystal wall there was a very small crack.

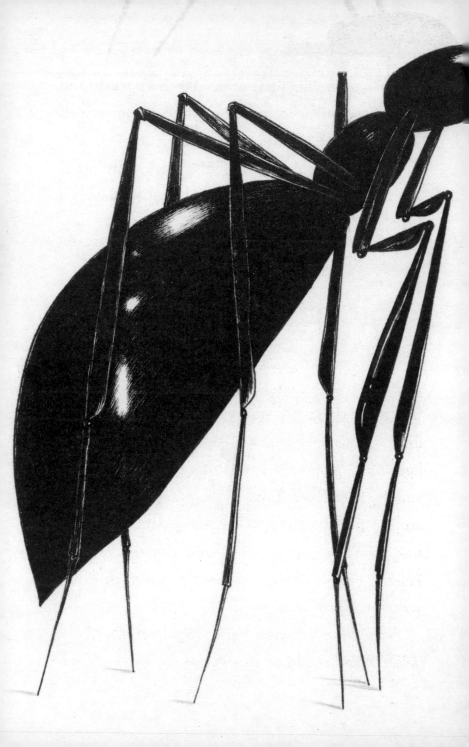

9

PRINCE OF ANTS

'I'll fight them off if they escape,' Peleus said, drawing his magic sword with a flash of silver lightning. 'You help that bird.' He struck a pose and menaced the fire devils, waving his blade around threateningly. But the fire devils took no notice. They just shrieked and capered harder. Peleus beat his chest with his free hand, uttering whooping war cries.

'Defy me at your peril, foul creatures,' he yelled. 'You shall not pass Peleus.'

'Poor little phoenix,' Antaeus crooned, lifting it down from the top of the ruby and tenderly laying it on the ground at Demon's feet as Peleus continued to shout defiantly behind them. Demon knelt beside it, stroking it gently. It was limp all over, its crest and tail drooping sadly and its eyes stuck together with a greyish-white film of gunk. When Demon gently opened its long beak to take a look inside, he found that the phoenix's throat was nearly clogged shut by a gloopy orange substance, which smelled hot and throat-chokingly bitter – like badly burnt caramel. Its thin, pointed tongue was covered in dark red pustules. Demon had never seen anything like it, and if he had wished for his magical medicine box to cure Arnie, he wished for it a million more times now. But realising that wishing wouldn't help, he pulled himself together. What he did have was Chiron's very own precious big *Book of Cures*. He got it out and put on his opticles.

'T for Throat,' he said, flicking through the pages frantically. Unfortunately the writing inside made no sense. He could read the letters, but it seemed to be set out in some sort of secret code.

Mix Merc. x 1 grain plus Hepar sulph. x 5 meas.

'What in Aphrodite's underpants does that mean?' he wailed. It was worse than the stupid language the medicine box used – he'd have to do his best to find a cure for the phoenix on his own. Scrabbling in the sack again, he pulled out everything he'd brought with him, thinking hard about what he'd learned from Chiron.

'This, this and . . . yes . . . this,' he said, dumping a few pinches of all the things he knew might work in a wooden bowl and pounding them together. Then he added a good dollop of the magic water and hoped.

Before he could get the bird to swallow, though, he had to put two fingers in and clear out the orange gloop. It was horrible and messy, and it burnt his skin, but finally it was done. He tipped in the throat mixture in small drops. The deep red pustules disappeared almost immediately, and the phoenix began to look a bit perkier. A little colour even started to return to its tail feathers, and then, all of a sudden, it hopped upright.

'You seem to be a healer after all, little shrimp,' said Antaeus. 'Though I'm sure most of it was my well water.'

'I don't mind what did it, as long as it works,' Demon said. 'Now for the eyes.' Putting together a different mixture of herbs, he made up a soothing milky potion with more of the magic water, then, taking a clean cloth, he gently bathed away the grey gunk till it was all gone. The phoenix blinked. There was still a grey film over its eyes, so Demon dripped some more of the mixture in. Slowly the grey cleared away until he could see the phoenix's beautiful golden irises and silver pupils, all surrounded by a circle of bright ruby red.

'You can see now, but can you sing?' Demon asked anxiously.

The phoenix cocked its head to one side and

opened its beak. A harsh croaking sound erupted from its throat.

'That sounds more like a dying crow than a song,' said Demon, trying not to despair. 'Let's try some more medicine.' But the bird shook its head, turning its beak away. It pointed one sharp claw and started to scratch something on the cave floor. Unfortunately, the claw made no impression on the shiny black stone.

'Are you trying to show me what will help?' Demon asked. The phoenix nodded.

'Here,' said Demon, holding out a pot of the white clay he used for making ointment. 'Try this.' The phoenix dipped its claw in the thick liquid and started to scratch again on the floor. Immediately, something began to take shape. Demon frowned. It couldn't be. But it was. The phoenix had drawn a gigantic ant.

'Is that an ant?' he asked. 'How can an ant help?' He turned to Antaeus, whose brown skin had now gone a kind of ashy grey. 'Do you know anything about ants?'

'Y-yes,' said the giant, not meeting Demon's eyes.

'Well?' Demon said impatiently.

'There's a nest of giant fire ants right on top of this mountain. They're called the Myrmex. I've never met them, though. They keep themselves to themselves.' Antaeus jerked the words out quickly, as if he didn't want to say them. It almost sounded as if he was afraid.

Demon turned back to the phoenix.

'Do you need one of the ants to come to you?' Demon asked the bird, but before he had finished, it was shaking its head from side to side and dipping its claw in the pot of clay again. This time, beside the ant, it drew a large circle with a smaller jagged circle within it, then tapped several times with its claw. It looked like a wonky dewdrop.

Demon scrubbed his hands through his hair, making it stand up on end. What could it mean? Just as he was about to ask Peleus what he thought, a sharp *crack* sounded behind him. Demon spun round as the fire devils' shrieks reached a new pitch.

'Oops!' said Peleus. There was now a long blade-shaped gash in the crystal, and a fresh crack had formed. The fire devils were scraping at it eagerly with their claws and blowing out more jets of white-hot flame.

'You idiot!' Antaeus and Demon roared at the same time. The phoenix let out another harsh croak, and started jumping up and down with rage, lunging weakly at Peleus with its beak.

'I'm sorry, I'm sorry,' he said, holding up a hand. 'My bad. I slipped.'

'Well, stop waving that thing around and come and help us figure this picture out,' said Demon. 'You're making things worse, not better.'

As soon as he saw the drawing of the giant-sized ant, and the circle beside it, Peleus smiled.

'Easy,' he said. 'That's a ball of ant nectar. Is that what you need, Phoenix?' The phoenix immediately stopped trying to skewer him with its beak, and nodded enthusiastically. 'Can you take us to the Myrmex, Antaeus?' Peleus went on. 'I think I can help get some.'

'Is this more of your stupid boasting?' Demon asked, still cross with the prince.

Peleus shook his head.

'No. I promise.'

But however much Demon pestered him, he would say no more on just how he intended to help.

Demon didn't want to leave the phoenix alone with the fire devils, but it shooed him out of the cave with its wings, croaking like a mad frog.

Once they were safely through the firefall again, Antaeus was very reluctant to take them to the peak of the mountain.

'Do you actually want us all to be burnt up by the fire devils?' Demon shouted at him.

Antaeus hung his huge head.

'No,' he said. But as they got near to the peak, which was sparkling golden pink in the early light, his lumbering run changed to a trot and then petered into a walk, whose steps got slower and slower. Suddenly, up ahead, Demon spotted a mass of segmented bright red ant bodies, feelers waving in the air. They were almost as big as the Giant Scorpion, and they were bobbing up and down, bowing to Helios's chariot as it drove over the eastern horizon, pulling the sun behind it.

Antaeus began to shake as he saw them.

'Ugh!' he said, his whole body shuddering till his armour rattled. 'Ugh! Ugh! Ugh! Too many legs! It's unnatural!' Dumping Demon and Peleus unceremoniously on the ground, he fled towards a nearby rock and cowered behind it. It didn't exactly hide his huge bulk.

Demon looked back at the giant, his mouth open. Now he understood. Antaeus was afraid of insects. He was about to ask Peleus what he thought they should do next when he realised the prince was no longer beside him.

Peleus was up ahead, dancing in and out of the ants, whirling around with his sword and making a strange clicking sound. The sword's silver blade caught the sun's rays, making a net of fiery lines in the air. Demon couldn't believe what he was seeing. The Myrmex were their only hope of saving the phoenix – and it looked like the prince was attacking them!

'You idiot!' he screamed at Peleus for the second time that day. 'You'll ruin everything!'

10

THE QUEEN'S MEDICINE

But even as the words left Demon's mouth, the ants started to dance with Peleus, making the same strange clicking sounds back at him. Demon soon realised that they were talking to each other – but despite his gift for understanding animals, he could only make out a few words, and those he could decipher didn't make much sense to him. Insect language was really hard – he'd only had the Giant Scorpion to practise on, and it didn't talk much. How did Peleus know ant language? How could he speak it?

There was no time to ask, though, because now Peleus was standing on the backs of two ants, looking like a young god, and clicking even louder, gesturing towards Demon with one hand. Before Demon knew what was happening, a pair of monstrous ant warriors were running towards him on their spindly legs. Their pincer jaws seized him, one under each armpit, and dragged him towards the huge mound of their nest.

'Help!' Demon cried out, trying to kick them. 'Let me go! Help! Peleus! What's going on? Antaeus! Save me!' But Peleus had disappeared into the round nest entrance, and Antaeus was still cowering behind his rock. As the ant jaws dug into the top of his shoulders like knives, Demon didn't dare say any more, afraid they would nip his dangling arms right off.

How could Peleus have betrayed Demon like this? And why? Was this all some mysterious plot to make him into ant food? A hot, angry tear ran down Demon's cheek. He'd really thought Peleus was his friend.

Deeper and deeper into the nest the giant ants ran, Demon's poor toes dragging and bumping along the floor. The network of strangely beautiful tunnels twisted and turned, so that Demon was soon giddy and completely lost. All he knew was that they were going downwards, and that the heat was getting unbearable, as was the dry, acrid smell of insect. Sweat dripped down his face, getting into his eyes, burning and stinging. The endless clicking of ant talk echoed through the nest.

'Please, Dad – please, great Pan – help me to understand them,' Demon whispered. Maybe if he knew what the ants were saying, he could learn to talk to them, explain that this was all a big mistake, tell them that all he wanted was some ant medicine for the poor phoenix, so it could sing its song. Wouldn't they all get burnt up too if the fire devils escaped? Surely they'd care about that.

Just then a breeze stroked his cheek, cool and green, smelling of forests and deep still pools.

My pipes! said a deep, moss-velvet voice inside Demon's head.

'Dad?' he gasped, trying to crane his head round. But Pan wasn't there. Cautiously, and with great difficulty, Demon managed to get his little finger inside his chiton, to where Pan's silver pipes were stowed. The effect was immediate. As soon as he touched them, he heard a loud, chittering chant.

'Hail to Peleus! Hail to the Prince of the Myrmidons!'

What in the name of Aphrodite's nightie are Myrmidons? he thought, just as his captors ran into a big open chamber crammed full of a seething swarm of insects and dropped him, sprawling, between the front legs of the biggest queen ant he'd ever seen. She was *twice* the size of her subjects, and her segmented red body glittered with golden specks.

Before he could get to his feet, Demon felt a hand at the back of his damp and sweaty chiton, pulling him up, and dusting him down. It was Peleus.

'You!' Demon hissed, his face turning a scarlet so furious that he thought he might burst into flames. 'What do you think you're doing?'

'Helping you get what you need,' said Peleus cheerfully. 'Now, *shh*!' Then he bowed low to the gigantic queen ant before Demon could say that he didn't want to *shh* one little bit.

'Your Majesty,' he said, in the clicking ant tongue. 'I bring you greetings from your human ant cousins, the Myrmidons, and from my father, their king. May your feelers ever prosper and your children number millions.'

His fingers still touching Pan's pipes, Demon's mouth fell open as he listened. Peleus's father was a king of human ants? He'd never mentioned that before. Well, that explained a few things!

'Greetings, Prince of Ants,' said the queen. 'And who is this small human you bring before me?' She bent forward, stroking her feelers over Demon's body till he had to bite his lip to stop from laughing. It felt very tickly. 'Is he a gift? Is he my breakfast?' As soon as Demon heard her say that, the urge to laugh left him very quickly, replaced by a cold wash of fear. He clenched his fists to stop them from trembling.

'This is Pandemonius, son of the great god Pan, and my friend and companion on a quest set by wise Athena,' said Peleus hurriedly. 'We need your help to save the phoenix and stop the fire devils escaping into the world.'

'And how may I do that?' the queen asked.

But before Peleus could answer, there was a great banging and shaking. As the floor trembled, Demon gasped. Had the fire devils escaped already? Was this the end? Were they all to be burnt up? He was sure he could feel the floor getting even hotter under his feet.

Suddenly he heard a familiar voice shouting. Antaeus had found his courage at last, and come to the rescue!

'Peleus! Demon! Where are you? Let me in!' yelled the giant, his gruff tones echoing through the nest, which shook from his repeated blows. With an enraged chittering and clicking, the ant warriors charged out of the queen's chamber and back towards the surface.

'Oh no!' said Peleus. 'Stupid giant! They'll kill him! I'd better go and tell him we're all right before he's stung to death.' He sprinted after the ant horde, leaving Demon alone with the queen and her attendants.

The queen tapped one pointy foot on the floor as Demon eyed her enormous pincer-like jaws. She could munch him up in an instant.

'Well?' she asked. 'What have you to say for yourself, small human?'

Demon took a deep breath, trying not to think of being eaten. 'Well, Your Majesty,' he said, stumbling a bit as he got his tongue round the difficult clicks. 'The phoenix thought you might have some special medicine.' He drew out a round shape in the air with his hands. 'In a ball. Nectar, Peleus called it.' He looked up into the queen's glittering eyes, willing her to help. 'If the fire devils escape, it will be a disaster. This mountain will be the first to burn. And if I can't cure the phoenix's voice so it can sing again, that's what will happen, and there's very little time left – the fire devil prison already has cracks in it.' His voice broke. 'It's . . . it's a real emergency, Your Majestic Antishness.'

The queen didn't waste any time. She turned to two of her attendants and clapped her front legs together. 'Fetch me two globes of sweet-acid nectar – at once,' she commanded. 'Hurry!' She looked down at Demon. 'If the Prince of Ants had not brought you, I should have considered you a juicy morning snack,' she said. 'You do know that, don't you?'

Demon nodded, just as the attendants scurried back, each carrying a round globe, full of a milky liquid. Now he felt ashamed of doubting Peleus. He was indeed a true friend.

'Thank you for not eating me, Your Majesty,' he said, tucking a globe carefully under each arm. They wobbled slightly, like jelly.

'Don't squash them,' said the queen sharply. 'They are a most precious gift. My ants took many days to make each one. Now go! I have no wish to be burnt up in my bed.'

Demon ran, as quickly as he dared, holding the globes as if they were delicate flowers. He didn't want the queen changing her mind.

11

PHOENIX SONG

As Demon emerged from the heat of the ant mound, he took in great gulps of fresh air. Antaeus and Peleus were waiting outside, surrounded by ant warriors. Antaeus still looked nervous, glancing around him with wild eyes, but his armour had obviously fended off the worst of the stings. Suddenly, the mountain itself gave a shudder. But this time it was not caused by Antaeus.

'Quick,' Demon said, his heart clenching with

dread. 'Down the mountain. We must get back to the phoenix.'

Antaeus scooped him and Peleus up at once, being extra-careful of the fragile sweet-acid globes.

'Goodbye, my ant brothers!' called Peleus to the warriors.

'Farewell, Prince of Ants,' they clicked back as the giant sprinted down the mountain so fast that the rocks became no more than a golden blur under his feet. Demon held his breath at each bump, willing the globes not to burst. He had no hands to cling onto Antaeus's ears with, so he had to trust the giant to keep him safe.

As they approached the phoenix's cave, the ground shuddered harder. This time Antaeus threw his feather cloak over both boys and rushed through the firefall. There was no time to waste. Burns would heal – but not if the phoenix wasn't saved.

The floor of the cave was rippling like tiny black waves and a thick smell of sulphur filled the air. A third, much larger crack had appeared in the crystal wall, and Demon was horrified to see that white-hot sparks were fizzing through it. The fire devils were screaming with triumph. It was a horrible sound. They were nearly free.

Demon jumped to the ground, almost falling on the unsteady floor in his panic to reach the phoenix.

'Steady,' said Peleus, quickly following him. 'Don't spill it!'

Demon didn't answer. He handed Peleus one globe before cracking the other in half, like an egg, and tipping the sweet-sour smelling liquid down the phoenix's gaping beak. One half went in, then the other.

'C'mon,' he whispered. 'C'mon! Work!'

For one agonising moment nothing seemed to be happening, then, all at once, the phoenix started to shine, all the way from beak to tail. Light poured out of its feathers in shades of flame from brightest citrine white to deepest tourmaline red, so bright that Demon had to cover his eyes. Its long tail feathers fanned out with a crisp snap, looking just like jade-gold lightning. Backing away, Demon took shelter under Antaeus's cloak, where Peleus was already crouched.

With a flap like a billowing sail, the phoenix's wings opened and it soared high up to the roof of the cave before swooping down to seize branch after branch. Almost quicker than the eye could see, it built its nest on top of the ruby, ignoring the enraged shrieking from the back of the cave, where even more white-hot sparks were escaping through the crystal wall.

'Hurry! Oh, do hurry!' Demon said, clutching Peleus's hand without even noticing. 'Oh, why doesn't it sing? What if the queen's medicine doesn't give the phoenix back its voice?'

Peleus squeezed his hand.

'It'll be all right,' he said. 'At least . . . I think it will. And we've got the other globe of nectar if we need to give it more.'

Soon the nest was finished. It was square and perfect, laced with berries, fruit, bark and flowers, which added flashes of colour. The phoenix settled itself on top and opened its beak. For a breathless moment everything was still. Demon crossed every finger and toe he had.

Then a note of diamond-pure sound erupted from the phoenix's long beak, followed by another, and another, dropping like tiny jewels through the sulphur-laden air. The Song of Renewal was so beautiful that afterwards both Demon and Peleus would always compare it to each piece of music they heard. Nothing ever came close to the wonder of the phoenix's song.

The fire devils were not so happy with its sound, though. They cowered back, their wailing high and shrill. Gradually, the cracks filled in and disappeared, and the crystal became less and less transparent. Soon it was so thick that no trace or sound of the fire devils could be seen or heard. They were safely trapped in their crystal prison for another hundred years. Still the phoenix sang on.

Gradually wisps of smoke began to rise from the wooden nest, and then flames.

'No!' Demon gasped, lurching forward. But Antaeus pulled him back with one ham-like hand.

'Hush!' he said. 'This must happen. Wait and see.'

As the giant spoke, the nest blazed up in a tall white pillar of fire. A delightful scent of cinnamon, frankincense and rose replaced the sulphur smell, and then, as suddenly as it had appeared, the column of flame was gone, and the phoenix with it.

A mass of fluttering phoenix feathers drifted through the air and the top of the ruby appeared to be completely empty. Demon looked round in panic. Oh no! Where had the bird gone? Had the fire killed it? But as the feathers cleared, he saw a large sapphire and gold egg, which began to rock back and forth.

Soon small cracks appeared in the shell, and Demon could hear a tapping sound.

'It's going to hatch,' said Peleus, rushing forward and dragging Demon behind him. 'Look!'

The egg burst open in a shower of jagged blue-gold pieces, revealing a small golden chick, which cheeped loudly. Before their astonished eyes, it grew and grew, until a full-sized phoenix stood before them again, tail trailing magnificently down the side of the ruby, its crest raised high.

'Ah!' it said, in a beautifully musical voice. 'That's more like it. It's always so cramped in my egg.'

'Are you all right?' Demon asked. He still couldn't quite believe what he'd just seen.

'Better than new,' it replied. 'Thank you for curing me, Pandemonius – and you too, young prince. I didn't think you'd make it back in time.'

'We nearly didn't,' said Demon. 'Luckily, Antaeus is fast.'

The phoenix cocked its head.

'I suppose you'll want more of my feathers for that cloak of yours, giant?' it said.

Antaeus nodded.

'Someone . . .' he gave a sideways look at Demon, 'someone pulled a whole lot out.'

Demon spluttered in protest. 'I was only trying to help,' he said.

Antaeus just gave his great, rumbling laugh and ruffled Demon's hair.

The phoenix fluttered down and picked up two feathers in its beak, before giving one each to Demon and Peleus.

'To thank you,' it said. 'Those few who belong to the Legion of Phoenix Protectors can call on me if they are ever in great need or danger, and I will come. Just throw the feather into a fire made of sandalwood, and say my name. Mind, though, it only works once.'

It nudged Demon's leg.

'Take that spare globe of ant nectar with you too,' it said. 'It might come in handy one day for a healer like you. Powerful stuff, that is. You'll know when to use it, I expect.'

With that, it stretched out its wings and soared away through the firefall with a melodious cry of farewell.

Demon repacked his medicine sack with a yawn, tucking the phoenix feather carefully inside Chiron's big *Book of Cures*.

'I suppose we'd better make a start on getting back,' he said.

On the way down the mountain, Peleus persuaded Antaeus to teach him to wrestle.

'Why do you heroes always have to be fighting?' Demon asked sleepily. He was tired and hungrier than a starving chimera.

'It's what we do,' said Peleus. 'Don't worry, Demon. I'll only use wrestling in an emergency.' He patted his hip. 'After all, I have my magic blade.' But Demon was snoring against Antaeus's shoulder and didn't hear.

At the bottom of the mountain, happy whinnying penetrated Demon's dreams. As he opened his eyes, he saw Keith and Sky Pearl frolicking round a familiar tall figure with an owl on her shoulder. The Goddess of Wisdom smiled a knowing smile as she heard the sound of three rumbling stomachs coming towards her. Athena snapped her fingers, and on the flowers at her feet there appeared a magnificent picnic, spread on a cloth of silver-embroidered purple spider silk. All Demon's favourite foods were there – honey cakes and apricot tarts, melting piles of roast lamb with garlicky gravy, crisp-skinned chickens bursting with juice and a whole pile of carrots baked with sesame seeds and honey, among many others. His mouth began to water, and he had to swallow hard to keep from dribbling like Doris the Hydra.

'Well done, Pandemonius,' Athena said, drawing him aside from the others as they fell on the food like starving wolves. 'Before you eat, I have a reward for you. A certain owl told me you'd like it.' Sophie hooted softly. The goddess reached into the air and drew out a beautiful book, bound in red leather and gold. Demon's eyes grew round as apples as he took it and opened it. It was full of creamy white blank pages.

'Oh,' he said, stroking its smoothness. 'It's perfect, Your Wise Wondrousness. It's so much better than my old slate! Now I can write my patient notes just like Chiron does.'

Athena laughed.

'I suggest you start with the case of the poorly phoenix,' she said.

'I shall, Your Celestial Cleverness,' he said, as she and Sophie disappeared in a flash of silver light.

'Hey, Demon,' said Peleus. 'Come and eat before Antaeus snaffles these delicious honey cakes.'

'Hands off!' said Demon happily. 'Those are all mine!'

GLOSSARY

BEASTS:

Basilisk *(BASS-uh-lisk):* King of the serpents. Every bit of him is pointy, poisonous, or perilous.

Bronze Bulls: Fire-breathing bovines Khalko and Kafto, who were created by Hephaestus for King Aeetes of Colchis.

Celestial Horses *(SELL-ess-tee-ul):* Giant stallions who pull Helios's chariot and the sun from east to west every day around the Earth.

Cerberus *(SER-ber-us):* Huge three-headed, snake-maned hound, Guardian of the Underworld, and Hades' favourite cuddly pet.

Colchian Dragon *(COL-chee-un):* Ares' smelly pet and Guardian of the Golden Fleece. Watch out for sparks if he farts . . . BOOOOM!

Cretan Bull *(KREE-tun)*: A furious, fire-breathing bull. Don't stand too close.

Griffin *(GRIH-fin)*: Couldn't decide if it was better to be a lion or an eagle, so decided to be both.

Hippocamps *(HIPPO-camps)*: Part horse, part fish. A sort of seahorse, if you like.

Hydra *(HY-druh)*: Nine-headed water monster. Hera somehow finds this loveable.

Ladon *(LAY-dun)*: A many-headed dragon that never sleeps (maybe the heads take turns?)

Medean Dragons: Two poison-spitting, biting beasts that pull the witch-princess Medea's chariot.

Minotaur *(MIN-uh-tor)*: A monster-man with the head of a bull. Likes eating people.

Myrmex *(MER-mex)*: Giant fire ants. Like sun-worshipping and dancing.

Nemean Lion *(NEE-mee-un)*: A giant, indestructible lion. Swords and arrows bounce off his fur.

Pegasi *(PEG-a-sigh)*: Mini flying horses with cute gold horns.

Phoenix *(FEE-nix)*: Wondrous bird with a burning desire to be reborn every 100 years.

Stymphalian Birds *(stim-FAY-lee-un)*: Man-eating birds with metal feathers, metal beaks and toxic dung.

Telchines *(TELL-keens)*: Underwater monsters with dog heads and seal flippers. Scary.

GODS AND GODDESSES:

Amphitrite *(AM-fih-TRY-tee)*: Sea Goddess and Poseidon's wife.

Aphrodite *(AF-ruh-DY-tee)*: Goddess of Love and Beauty and all things pink and fluffy.

Ares *(AIR-eez)*: God of War. Loves any excuse to pick a fight.

Athena *(a-THEE-na)*: Goddess of Wisdom and defender of pesky, troublesome heroes.

Artemis *(AR-te-miss)*: Goddess of the Hunt. Can't decide if she wants to protect animals or kill them.

Boreas *(BOH-ree-as)*: Icy God of the North Wind. Carries a handy bag of bouncy breezes.

Chiron *(KY-ron)*: Centaur God – part horse, part man – brother of Zeus and humungously awesome healer of all ills.

Dionysus *(DY-uh-NY-suss)*: God of Wine. Turns even sensible gods into silly goons.

Eos *(EE-oss)*: Goddess of the Dawn. Married to Tithonus, a grasshopper.

Eros *(EAR-oss)*: Mischievous young love god who likes playing with hearts.

Eris *(AIR-iss)*: Goddess of Discontent. Argumentative, likes war and blood a bit too much.

Hades *(HAY-deez)*: Zeus's youngest brother and the gloomy Ruler of the Underworld.

Helios *(HEE-lee-us)*: The bright, shiny and blinding God of the Sun.

Hephaestus *(Hih-FESS-tuss)*: God of Blacksmithing, Metal, Fire, Volcanoes, and everything awesome.

Hera *(HEER-a)*: Zeus's scary wife. Drives a chariot pulled by screechy peacocks.

Hermes *(HER-meez)*: Mischievous Messenger God with a handy invisibility hat and winged sandals.

Hestia *(HESS-tee-ah)*: Goddess of the Hearth and Home. Bakes the most heavenly treats.

Iris *(EYE-riss)*: Goddess of the Rainbow and messenger of the gods. Also a slightly sick-making form of transport between Olympus and Earth. Seatbelts, please!

Persephone *(per-SEF-oh-nee)*: Goddess of Spring, stolen away by Hades to be his wife. Made bad mistake of eating pomegranate seeds in the Underworld.

Poseidon *(puh-SY-dun)*: God of the Sea and controller of supernatural events.

Zeus *(ZOOSS)*: King of the Gods. Fond of smiting people with lightning bolts.

OTHER MYTHICAL BEINGS

Antaeus *(an-TAY-ee-us)*: Superstrong giant and hero-killer. Collector of skulls.

Arachne *(ar-AKK-nee)*: Brilliant weaver. Turned into a spider by Athena for boasting about her skill. Oops.

Asclepius *(ass-KLEEP-ee-us)*: Healer apprentice to Chiron and the first ever doctor.

Autolycus *(AW-toe-lie-CUSS)*: A very naughty boy. Stole some cattle and blamed it on Heracles.

Cherubs *(CHAIR-ubs)*: Small flying babies. Mostly cute.

Dryads *(DRY-ads)*: Tree spirits. Only slightly more serious than nymphs.

Endeis *(en-DAY-ees)*: Chiron's daughter and oread of Mount Pelion. Also Peleus's mum.

Epimetheus *(ep-ee-MEE-thee-us)*: Prometheus's silly brother who designed animals. Thank him for giving us the platypus and naked mole rat.

Eurydice *(YOUR-id-ee-see)*: Tree-nymph and all-time greatest love of Orpheus. Stepped on a snake by mistake. Died.

Geryon *(JAYR-ee-un)*: A cattle-loving Giant with a two-headed dog.

Heracles *(HAIR-a-kleez)*: The half-god 'hero' who was given twelve impossible tasks by scary Hera, including stealing poor Cerberus from the Underworld and dragging him up to Earth. Loooves killing magical beasts.

Jason *(JAY-sun)*: Fleece-stealing hero, basher of bulls and captain of the good ship *Argo*.

Lethe *(LEE-thee)*: Memory-stealing spirit of forgetfulness. Lives in a marsh.

Medea *(Med-EE-ah)*: Tricksy witch-princess, dragon-owner and girlfriend of Jason.

Maenads *(MAY-nads)*: Followers of Dionysus, lovers of dancing and partying.

Myrmidons *(MER-mid-ons)*: Fierce ant-soldier subjects of Peleus's dad, King Aeacus of Aegina.

Naiads *(NYE-ads)*: Water spirits. Keeping Olympus clean and refreshed since 500 BC.

Nereids *(NEAR-ee-ids)*: Sea nymphs (girls) – their brothers are Nerites. Daughters of Nereus, the Old Man of the Sea.

Nereus *(NEH-re-us)*: The Old Man of the Sea, a shapeshifter fond of wrestling heroes like Heracles.

Nymphs *(NIMFS)*: Giggly, girly, dancing nature spirits.

Oread *(Or-AY-ad)*: Mountain nature spirit (see Endeis).

Orpheus *(or-FEE-us)*: Magnificent musician who tried to rescue his beloved Eurydice from the Underworld. (Massive fail there, then.)

Pandora *(pan-DOR-ah)*: The first human woman. Accidentally opened a jar full of evil.

Peleus *(PEL-ee-us)*: Chiron's boastful hero grandson and prince of Aegina. Likes swishing swords about.

Prometheus *(pruh-MEE-thee-us)*: Gave fire to mankind, and was sentenced to eternal torture by bird-pecking.

Satyrs *(SAY-ters)*: 50% goat, 50% human. 100% party animal.

Silenus *(sy-LEE-nus)*: Dionysus's best friend. Old and wise, but not that good at beast-care.

Tritons *(TRY-tuns)*: Half man, half two-tailed fish.

PLACES:

Aegina (*eye-GEE-na*): Island ruled by Peleus's dad and mum. Home of the Myrmidons.

Aeolia (*ay-OH-lee-ah*): Ancient name for Thessaly, an area of central Greece and bloody battleground of Ares and Eris.

Arcadia (*ar-CAY-dee-a*): Wooded hills in Greece where the nymphs and dryads like to play.

Macriss (*MACK-riss*): Large seahorse-shaped island off the Greek coast where Poseidon has his second palace.

Mount Pelion (*PEE-lee-on*): Mountain in Northern Greece and happy home of Chiron the centaur and his apprentices.

Tartarus (*TAR-ta-russ*): A delightful torture dungeon miles below the Underworld.

The Underworld: Hades' happy little kingdom of dead people, also known as Hell in Northern parts.